YOUNG NOAH
EAGLE EYE

FORWARD

THE IDEA FOR THIS BOOK INITIALLY CAME ABOUT IN THE EARLY 2000'S.
I APPROACHED ERIC (THE AUTHOR) ABOUT A YOUNG NOAH BOOK SERIES AND AFTER MANY YEARS, DELAYS AND SIDE ROADS, YOUNG NOAH WAS BORN.

HAVING ATTENDED GRAD SCHOOL AND OBTAINING A DEGREE IN MENTAL HEALTH COUNSELING, I WAS CONTINUALLY REMINDED OF MY OWN STRUGGLES WITH DYSLEXIA AND ADHD WHICH GREATLY AFFECTED MY ABILITY TO LEARN.

THE TREMENDOUS FEAR AND TOXIC SHAME I SUFFERED ASSOCIATED WITH SCHOLASTIC DIFFICULTIES AND EMBARRASSINGS SOCIAL INTERACTION DROVE ME TO EXCESSIVE PARTYING IN MY TEEN YEARS TO COPE WITH THE PAIN.

GOD IN HIS MERCY INTERVENED IN THE MIDST OF MY HARDEST STRUGGLES AND REVEALED HIS LOVE AND PLAN OF SALVATION TO ME THROUGH HIS SON YESHUA (JESUS) AT 21 YEARS OF AGE.

FROM FIRSTHAND EXPERIENCE, I REALIZED THAT YOUNG CHILDREN SOMETIMES HAVE GREAT DIFFICULTY EXPRESSING STRONG NEGATIVE FEELINGS ABOUT WHAT THEY ARE BATTLING WITH. YOUNG NOAH'S PURPOSE, I BELIEVE, IS TO BRING CHILDREN ENGAGING STORIES OF CONQUERING FEARS AND DISABILITY STIGMAS THROUGH THE CHALLENGED ANIMALS HELPED BY YOUNG NOAH.

YOUNG NOAH, IMAGINED AS A CHILD HIMSELF, IS DIVINELY GIFTED TO SEE AND SOLVE EACH ANIMAL'S DILEMMA THROUGH FOCUSSED PROBLEM-SOLVING AND INSPIRED INSIGHT.

APPROACHING PROBLEMS FROM DIFFERENT PERSPECTIVES, HEALING THROUGH COMPASSIONATE UNDERSTANDING AND EMBRACING TRUTH IS THE HALLMARK OF THIS PLANNED BOOK SERIES.

C W PARRY MA   JUNE 2020

YOUNG NOAH

EAGLE EYE

For information contact:
Eric McConnell **YOUNGNOAHADVENTURES.COM**-
Written and illustrated by
Eric McConnell Story idea by CW Parry MA
Cover and interior design by Eric McConnell

Library of Congress Catalogue-In-Publishing
Data is available
Printed in the United States of America
10 9 8 7 6 65 4 3 2 1
First Edition: JUNE 2020

YOUNG NOAH

EAGLE EYE

WRITTEN AND ILLLUSTRATED BY

ERIC MCCONNELL

STORY / IDEA BY

CW PARRY, MA

"COME TO ME, ALLWHO ARE WEARY AND BURDENED, ANDI WILL GIVE YOU REST. TAKE MY YOKE UPON YOU AND LEARN FROM ME, FOR I AM GENTLE AND HUMBLE IN HEART, AND YOU WILL FIND REST FOE YOUR SOULS. FOR MY YOKE IS EASY AND MY BURDEN IS LIGHT."   MATTHEW 11: 28-30

CHAPTERS

CHAPTER 1.

SURPRISE MORNING

Thousands of years ago in the ancient world, mornings were beautiful and bright.
Young Noah and his best friend, Bronnie had decided to travel through the lush forest opening up at the water's edge.

It was calm and beautiful on the beach at that time of day with life and activity beginning to stir everywhere.

Because the inland sea's surface was calm, colorful fish could be seen darting around just beneath the water's surface.

Cliff-dwelling eagles took the opportu-
nity to hunt and catch leaping fish that
were looking for food.
Noah and Bronnie watched from the beach
as a young eaglet who had just learned to
fly, attempt to catch a fish as it jumped
out of the water.

This eaglet's eyesight was dim and it missed the fish, instead crashing into the water.

Noah and Bronnie looked on shocked and concerned as the eaglet thrashed about, being weighed down by his soaked feathers.

The eaglet screeched, "Aaaaggghh! Help me! I can't swim!"
"We have to get to him before he drowns!" said Noah to Bronnie.
"Yes! Let's wade out until the water is too deep for you, then climb onto my back." Bronnie directed.

Noah and Bronnie hurriedly waded out
into the shallow water. Now with Noah
on Bronnie's back, they approached the
struggling eaglet. Noah reached down and
scooped him up, drenched and frightened.

"You're going to be okay, little guy!
We've got you."
Noah carefully pressed the water off the
eaglet's wings and body, while attempting
to dry him the best that he could.
"Thank you for helping me. I thought I
was going to drown!"

"Why did you fly into the water?" asked
Noah.
"It was an accident!" Screeched the
eaglet, hoping Noah would understand.

"I can't see well, which is unusual for
eagles, because we're supposed to have
the best eyesight of all.
The fish jumped out of the water, but I
was too late and I missed him."

Noah sensed what he'd said and that the
eaglet was very disappointed in himself.
"Where do you live?"

The eaglet directed his gaze upward toward the cliffs overlooking the water.

"Up at the top of the cliffs overlooking the water. I come from a tribe of Royal Emperor Eagles that have hunted here for hundreds of years." the eaglet tried to tell Noah.

"You're really special!" Exclaimed Noah.

"Well, my father the emperor doesn't think so. He's upset with me because I have trouble hunting and everything is blurry. He just doesn't understand how hard I try..."

"So you keep crashing because you can't see well?" Asked Noah.

CHAPTER 2

UNEXPECTED TREASURE

"Yes! I overheard my father and mother talking when they didn't know I was there. My father told my mother that he didn't think I'd ever be able to lead the eagle tribe." The eaglet's pained face seemed to say.

"He's mad at me a lot and I don't know
what to do."
Noah suggested,
"I think we first need to get him home,
right, Bronnie?'
"Yes, indeed." Replied Bronnie.

"Young eagle, we will be happy to take you with us up to the top of the cliffs, though it is quite a long, steep climb."

The young eagle thought to himself: "Yes, thank you,I'd..."

Suddenly, a swiftly-moving shadow glides across the water and casts an ominous dark image over the group. A piercing "SCREEECH!" startles them and then <u>swoop!</u> The little eaglet is abruptly grabbed and carried up into the air by a huge, fierce eagle.

"Aaaahh!" Screams the eaglet.
Noah and Bronnie watch him get carried away toward the seaside cliffs by his Emperor Eagle father. He abruptly dropped the wet and distressed eaglet into the large eagle's nest set on the edge of the cliff.

The eaglet landed in the nest with a thud.
The father eagle snaps at him angrily, "No more foolishness! You've embarrassed me long enough and I'm bringing you home. You're grounded!"

Noah is upset. "We've got to help him!
He's isolated and alone with no one to
talk to.
Maybe we can figure out something to help
him see better!"

Bronnie thought of something as they walked along the beach.
"Hmmm.   So, Young Noah, do you have any ideas?"
"Umm, I sure don't." Replied Noah.

"What have you done in the past when these types of problems arise and you don't know what to do?"
Bronnie asked him.
Noah ponders for a second. Then an expression of relief washed over his face.

"Oh yeah. We need to ask God what to do."
Bronnie laughs, "I was wondering how long
it would take for you to see that."
"Lord God, please show us a way to help
that young eagle. He can't see well and
it makes his father so angry. Please
help!" Prayed Noah.

Time passed as they walked, but then a bright glare relecting the sun's light shone up from the water's edge, catching their attention.
A translucent stone, clear as glass, had been deposited on the sand by a gently lapping tide.

"Whoa! What's this?" Said Noah.
"It's the clearest, brightest stone I've ever seen!" Exclaimed Bronnie.
Noah held the stone up to his eye to look through for himself.

He then held it up for Bronnie to look
through. They noticed that everything
looked bigger when viewed through it.
Noah was amazed.
"I've never seen things this big and
clear before!"

CHAPTER 3

BRILLIANT IDEA

"I wonder if it could be used to help the eagle see better? Bring it back to your workshop and let's see what can be done." Suggested Bronnie.
The two walked the short distance back to Noah's workshop at his family's home.

"That stone covers both your eyes. Wait!
What if you carefully cut the stone in
half and attached them to fit each of the
eagle's eyes?
A frame could be created to hold them
together." Offered Bronnie.

Noah liked the idea.
"Yes! And it would fit his head somehow.
Umm...maybe a strap tying them to his
head could keep them from falling off.
Great idea, Bronnie!"
Noah went to work, carefully cutting the
clear stone into halves with a chisel-

-and smoothing out the rough edges.
With Bronnie's guidance, Noah attached
the two clear stone halves together with
a solid wooden pin. Additional strong
wooden rails on each side of the halves
made a wearable frame.

"Look! Everything is clearer now! Maybe this will help the eagle see better! Let's try to find him." said Noah.
"He's up at the top of the cliffs over-looking the sea. It will be quite a journey to reach him." Replied Bronnie.

"Yes!" Said Noah. "Let's both go to the foot of the mountain leading up to his nest. I'll climb the steep part by myself."
Bronnie and Noah arrived at the base of the cliff and the steep climb up.

Noah journeyed to the eaglet alone, carrying the glasses he'd made in a satchel along with his staff.

The eaglet looked very sad as Noah approached him.

"Hello, little eagle, remember me? I came here to help you!"

The eaglet pouts, thinking to himself: "How can you help me? I'm just no good at flying well and now my father's mad and says I'm grounded!"
Understanding his predicament, Noah pulls out the glasses he'd made for the eaglet from his satchel.

Noah demonstrates the glasses by trying them on.
"What's that?" The troubled eaglet's expression seemed to say.
Noah gently set the glasses on the bridge of the eaglet's beak.
Wow!

The eaglet was amazed.
Suddenly everything around him became
sharp and clear like never before.
Noah was careful to anchor the glasses in
place by fastening them with a leather
strap to the eaglet's head.

Noah gestures to the cliff's edge. "Why don't you try it out? You already know how to fly, but now you'll see everything much better than before and won't crash!"
The eaglet looked up at Noah nervously.

Now with keen eyesight, the little eagle
looked down and -gulps!-
Thinking to himself: "I-I don't know if I
can do this!" He pauses.
Noah was aware of his fear and offered
more encouragement.
"I know you'll do great!"

CHAPTER 4

DANGEROUS FLIGHT

Instinctively, the eaglet knew Noah was
right.
Summoning all his royal eagle's courage,
he unfurled his wings and leaped off the
cliff's edge, letting the gentle updraft
float him out over the rocks and water.

He was free and he could see!
Noah shouted, "Amazing! I knew you could
do it!"
The eaglet looked back over his shoulder
at Noah to give him a big smile.
Noah watched him fly far out over the
forest toward the distant mountains.

The eaglet was overjoyed, thinking, "Now
I can see! And maybe I can hunt and fish
without messing up and my father will be
proud of me!"
With new confidence, the eaglet ventured
farther than he'd ever flown before.
Volcanoes rose up in the distance.

Noah climbed back back down to meet Bronnie, who was pleased.
"It looks like the eaglet has discovered
flying again for the first time!
He was scared at first, but once he over-
came his fear of failing, he now sees who
he really is!"

"I just hope his eagle father isn't angry
at him for leaving the nest."
Said Bronnie to Noah.
The eaglet's parents returned to the
abandoned nest.
They were surprised to see it empty,

especially after their son had been told he'd been grounded.

The Emperor Eagle was angry. "Not only is that son of yours incapable of becoming the eagle who can replace my leadership someday, but he's defiant and rebellious! He's really in trouble now!"

The young eagle began noticing that the
lush greenery had been replaced by a
blackened and charred landscape scented
with the smell of sulphur. Yuck!
The eaglet thought,
"I've never flown this far from home!"

"Why have all the green plants and trees
disappeared? I'm tired and
I need to rest. But where?
Ahh! There's an old tree..."
He landed carefully on the barren branch
of a dead tree.

The eaglet was uneasy seeing that everything around him was desolate and void
of life. He began to remember the angry
reprimand he'd gotten from his father.
He felt depressed.

Bronnie confided to Noah, "Something isn't right. The birds have stopped chirping and it seems strangely quiet."

"Hmm. Yes, I sense the same thing." Acknowledged Noah.

Having stopped briefly at a large clearing, first Bronnie and now Noah realized that something didn't feel right. The usual buzz of insects and flitting of birds had ceased. They looked around. Then, suddenly...

(A growing rumbling, ground shaking)

"W-whaat's that? Do you feel that?"
said Noah.
The low rumbling and shaking of the
ground intesified.

"Yes!" Agreed Bronnie.

KA-BOOM! A distant but loud explosion caused them both to flinch.
Bronnie reacted, alarmed.
"That's a volcano exploding! This has happened before. All the animals in the forest are in danger!"

Back at the lava field, the force of the explosion knocked the eaglet off the tree branch. Terrified, he turned to see what had been a mountain now spewing black smoke and flaming boulders the size of houses in all directions.

A river of molten lava flowed from the now blown-off top of the mountain, rushing right at him.
The eaglet dodged monstrous flying, flaming rocks that narrowly missed him.
"Ohh nooo!' He cried.

CHAPTER 5

ESCAPE TO FREEDOM

Reaching the outer edge of the forest, he flew to avoid firey projectiles crashing all around him.
The eaglet took one look back at the flam-ing boulders and flood of lava invading the land, driving him to fly even faster.

On the forest floor, the smaller animals
reacted to the thunderous explosion of
the volcano.
They turned and fled in terror, confused,
not sure where to run.

The stampede grew larger and larger, from the least of them to the greatest. The animals panicked, barely keeping ahead of the rapidly flowing lava tearing through the forest.

The eaglet, flying directly above them,
screeched loudly,
"Run! RUN! A mountain has exploded and
it's raining fire! Follow me to the sea!"
The animals followed him as he guided
them to safety.

As the eaglet first appeared over the tree-
tops and into the clearing, a stampede of
animals following him rushing from the dense
undergrowth.
"It's the young eagle!
He rescued the animals!" Said Bronnie.

Now far enough away from danger, the forest animals poured into the open area. Though all were shaken, the smaller ones were drawn to Noah and Bronnie, explaining what had happened to them in excited gibberish.

But Noah understood what they were trying to say. The animals all acknowledged the eaglet as the one who had guided them to safety.
"We were so scared!
If it wasn't for the eagle guiding us, we wouldn't have known where to go when the volcano erupted!" They seemed to say.

"I barely escaped the volcano and then saw all the animals. I called to them to follow me out of the forest!"

Noah recognized that the eaglet had directed the fleeing animals to follow him.

Noah congratulated him.
"Because of you, many more of them sur-
vived who would have perished. You're a
hero!"
The eaglet soaked up the compliment and
attention. It made him feel valuable and

worthwhile. Then, an ominous shadow
crossed over the group. They all looked
up to see the emperor eagle flying over-
head.
He desended quickly, landing on a log
next to his son.

CHAPTER 6

RECONCILED

"What's all this?
And why did you leave the nest when I
told you that you were grounded?
What are those strange, clear stones on
your face?"
The emperor eagle scolded.

"And WHO are THEY?"
The emperor eagle demanded, indicating
all the animals and Noah.
Noah understood the father eagle's confu-
sion and spoke up for the eaglet.
"Your son is a brave eagle." Noah said

to the emperor eagle.
"He escaped a deadly volcano and led all these animals out of the forest to safety. These clear stones help him to see, where he was almost blind before."

"He needs your encouragement and sup-
port."
Noah looked intently at the father eagle.
Though not understanding human words, he
knew what Noah had meant. He now felt
regret for being so harsh with his son.

The emperor eagle apologized to him.
"Son, I've been very hard on you. It
wasn't right. Now I know you had difficulty seeing and I didn't fully understand. I'm very proud of you for being
so brave. Please forgive me."

"I forgive you, father.
I've just always wanted you to be proud
of me."
Said the eaglet to his father.
"I am, son.
I was the one who was blind."

The volcanos' rumbling stopped.
Out of harm's way from the flood of lava,
all the animals said goodbye to the young
eagle and started to head back to their
forest homes.
"Our prayers were answered."
Said Bronnie to Noah.

"Yes! God did so much more than we ex-
pected!" Exclaimed Noah.
"Let's go home."
Said the father eagle to the eaglet.
The father eagle turned and took flight,
beckoning his son to follow him.

Noah and Bronnie watched as father and son joyfully flew home together to the nest in the cliffs. They saw the mending of a broken relationship and new confidence begun in a brave young eagle destined to lead his tribe.

"Do you think we'll see him again?"
Asked Bronnie.

"I'm sure we will."
Noah said hopefully.

"But next time he'l be carrying a fish as big as he is!" Joked Noah.

They both laughed.

THE END

ACKNOWLEDGEMENTS

FOR THE INVALUABLE CONTRIBUTIONS TO THE WRITING AND PUTTING TOGETHER OF THIS BOOK, I WANT TO FIRST THANK MY MOM AND DAD, GERALDINE AND GEORGE MC CONNELL.
BOTH ARTISTS THEMSELVES, THEY CONTINUALLY ENCOURAGED MY CREATIVE PROCESS AND PURSUITS THROUGHOUT CHILDHOOD AND MY LIFE.
BOTH GIFTED PAINTERS, I GREATLY ADMIRED THEIR LEVEL OF SKILL AND SOUGHT TO EMULATE THEM FROM AN EARLY AGE.

MY CLOSE FRIEND CRAIG PARRY, WHO ORIGINATED THE IDEA OF YOUNG NOAH IN THE EARLY 2000'S AND CONVINCED ME TO PURSUE THE CHARACTER AND STORYLINE POSSIBILITIES.

LIKE ME, CRAIG ENDURED MORE THAN HIS SHARE OF OSTRACISM, RIDICULE AND REJECTION. THIS INSPIRED HIM TO BECOME A MENTAL HEALTH COUNSELOR AND HELP OTHERS IN THEIR BATTLE WITH THE SAME STRUGGLES.   HIS CONTRIBUTION TO THE CORE OF THIS BOOK'S CONTENT MADE IT POSSIBLE.

FINALLY, I WANT TO THANK MY LORD AND SAVIOR JESUS CHRIST, WHO GAVE HIS LIFE FOR ME THAT I COULD TRULY KNOW GOD AND HIS INCREDIBLE LOVE FOR ME.   HE IS THE SOURCE OF THE INSPIRATION FOR THE YOUNG NOAH STORIES AND THEIR INTENDED PURPOSE FOR HELPING CHILDREN EVERYWHERE COPE WITH LIFE'S CHALLENGES.

CPSIA information can be obtained
at www.ICGtesting.com
Printed in the USA
LVHW050746170920
666168LV00005B/19